THE BEGGAR
IN THE BLANKET

& Other Vietnamese Tales

DIAL BOOKS | NEW YORK

THE BEGGAR IN THE BLANKET
& Other Vietnamese Tales

retold by Gail B. Graham

illustrated by Brigitte Bryan

To Miss Ruthe and Mister Roger
and everyone at The Three R's School

CONTENTS

AUTHOR'S NOTE

I discovered the varied and little-known world of Vietnamese folktales during my first trip to Vietnam in 1966. When I returned to Vietnam early in 1967, I spent hours in Saigon libraries and bookstalls perusing the many French-language storybooks, elementary school readers, and other sources that were available to me. I came home with dozens of delightful stories and legends.

Vietnamese folktales have a personality of their own. A little magazine called The Vietnam Observer *reveals that "Most Vietnamese stories spring from the rural areas where life is not ruled by clocks and where children rest in the hot mid-day and stay up late in the evening. Story-telling is therefore often like an unwound ball of cord rolled under the stoop, around the areca palm, across the garden, tangled in a betel vine and with its end, if one is fortunate enough to get that far, quite possibly to be found in the middle of a rice paddy or in the stomach of a fish. Even then the story may not stop, the children are not yet sleepy, the air is cool and grandfather's ball of cord may just continue. The fish could suddenly turn to jade, be carved into the form of a boy who suddenly comes to life! . . ."*

The tales in this book are my favorites, written for my own children and for all children everywhere who love a good story.

GAIL B. GRAHAM
July, 1969

THE BEGGAR
IN THE BLANKET

& Other Vietnamese Tales

THE BEGGAR IN THE BLANKET

Many hundreds of years ago, two brothers lived in a village at the edge of the forest. Their names were Kim and De.

Kim was the elder, and he was very industrious. He had worked hard all his life, and now he was one of the richest men in the village.

De was inclined to be lazy. He worked when he needed something to eat or a new pair of sandals, but he never worked very hard and he never worked for very long. He lived all alone because he couldn't afford to feed a wife.

Kim had a number of friends who were as rich and as hard-working as he was. Kim's friends kept him so busy that he hardly ever had time to think about his poor, lazy younger brother.

But Kim's wife was a gentle and thoughtful woman, and she felt sorry for De.

"It's been more than a month since we've seen your brother," she said to Kim one night. "Why don't you ask him to come and have dinner with us?"

Kim was surprised. "What would Nguyen and Ton and Cao and Duc and all my other friends think if they came in and found that good-for-nothing brother of mine sitting at our table?" he asked. "They would be insulted! They would never come to my house again!"

"So much the worse for them," replied his wife. "Friends are not the same as a brother."

"And it's a good thing they're not!" Kim retorted. "The whole village would starve if all my friends were as lazy as De."

Kim's wife could see that it was no use arguing with her stubborn husband. Nevertheless she vowed that she would make Kim understand the value of a brother, even a poor and lazy brother like De.

The next evening Kim came home to find his wife weeping and trembling.

"A terrible thing has happened," she sobbed. "While you were away, a beggar came to our door and tried to rob us. I chased him with my broom, and he dropped his sack and tried to run away. But he stumbled over a stick of wood, and he fell . . . and he hit his head against the hearthstone. He's . . . he's dead."

Kim was horrified. "Where is he?"

His wife pointed toward the corner. "I wrapped him up in that old blanket," she said. "It wasn't my fault! He

13

was trying to rob us. But the Mandarin will never believe me; he'll think that I murdered a helpless old beggar! We are ruined!" And she wept harder than ever.

Kim sat down and tried to think. He thought and thought, but all he could think about was the terrible humiliation of having to go before the Mandarin and admit that his wife had killed a poor old beggar.

"*I* have an idea," Kim's wife said at last. "If you get one of your friends to help you, you can carry the beggar into the forest and bury him. No one will miss an old beggar, and even if they do, they won't think to suspect us."

Kim couldn't think of a better plan, so he snatched up his coat and hurried away to seek help from his friend Nguyen.

14

Nguyen listened politely to everything Kim said. But when Kim asked for help, Nguyen shook his head.

"I'd *like* to help you," he replied slowly. "But you see, I am so old and so weak that I really wouldn't be any help at all. Why don't you go and ask Ton?"

Kim crossed the road and rapped at Ton's door.

"Kim!" exclaimed Ton. "I was just thinking about you. Come in. Will you have a cup of tea?"

"I need your help," said Kim. And he explained what had happened.

As Kim spoke, Ton began to squirm and grimace as if he were in pain. At last Ton collapsed onto the floor. He drew his knees up to his chin and moaned.

"If only you had come at some other time!" groaned Ton. "I'd be happy to help you, but I've got terrible pains in my stomach! I'm much too sick to carry any-thing!"

Kim walked out into the night. I'll go and see Cao, he thought. Surely he will help me.

But Cao's house was dark and still. Cao and his whole family had gone to the next village for a visit.

It's a good thing I have so many friends, thought Kim. Duc will be home, and I know I can count on *him*.

Lights glowed in all the windows of Duc's house. Duc himself opened the door and bade Kim come in and warm himself by the fire.

Kim told Duc about the beggar. Duc was very sympathetic and understanding. He agreed that Kim's wife was not to blame, and he thought that the plan to bury the beggar in the forest was a very clever plan.

16

"Then you'll help me!" cried Kim.

Duc looked surprised. "Help you? Oh, I can't possibly help you," he said quickly. "You see, my wife isn't feeling very well this evening, and I don't want to leave her alone in the house."

There was nothing for Kim to do but return home and tell his wife that not one of his friends would help him.

"Fine friends!" she snorted. "They'll come to your house and eat your rice and drink up your tea, but where are they when you need them? It's a lucky thing for us that you have a brother! Don't just stand there, go and fetch De!"

Kim blinked. "Why should De be willing to help me?" he asked his wife. "What have I ever done for him?"

17

"Little enough," she replied. "But he's your brother. If he won't help you, no one will."

Much to Kim's surprise, De readily agreed to help him bury the beggar. The two brothers carried the rolled-up blanket deep into the forest and buried it beneath a tree. Then they went home to bed.

Kim's wife woke him at dawn.

"Kim!" she whispered. "There are three messengers from the Mandarin at our door!"

Kim dressed hurriedly and went out to see what the messengers wanted.

"You and your wife must come with us," said the first messenger.

"You have been summoned to appear before the Mandarin," said the second messenger.

18

"Make haste!" warned the third messenger. "The Mandarin must not be kept waiting!"

Kim and his wife marched obediently along behind the three messengers to the Mandarin's palace. They were led into a small bare chamber and told to wait. An hour passed. At last Kim and his wife were ordered to enter the Mandarin's court.

Nguyen and Ton and Duc were already there, standing at either side of the Mandarin's throne. Kim's heart sank. He knew in an instant that his friends had betrayed him.

The Mandarin looked sternly down at Kim.

"Your wife murdered a helpless beggar," said the Mandarin. "Last night you went to the homes of each of these three honest men and tried to persuade them to help you hide the beggar's body."

19

Kim stared at the floor and said nothing.

"These three honest men followed you into the forest," continued the Mandarin. "They watched you bury the beggar beneath a tree. And then they dug up the body and brought it here to me."

Four servants came forward and placed the rolled-up blanket at the Mandarin's feet.

"Unroll the blanket!" commanded the Mandarin.

It was done. A murmur of surprise swept through the room. For there was no beggar inside the blanket! Instead it was filled with sticks and stones.

The Mandarin glared at Nguyen and Ton and Duc. "You swore that this man and his wife had murdered a helpless beggar!" he said angrily. "You claimed a reward. Well, where is the beggar?"

Nguyen and Ton and Duc were silent.

"*Where is the beggar?*" thundered the Mandarin.

Kim's wife stepped forward and bowed. "Your Excellency," she said. "There *is* no beggar. I invented the story because I wanted to prove to my husband that the love of his poor brother was more valuable than the love of his rich friends."

The Mandarin was so impressed with her cleverness and so pleased that there hadn't been a murder that he bade all of them go back to their village. But Nguyen and Ton and Duc were so ashamed of themselves that they could scarcely hold their heads up. And Kim never forgot the lesson that he had learned from the beggar in the blanket.

21

THI KINH

Thi Kinh was very beautiful. Her black hair was long and fragrant, and her big, dark eyes sparkled like living stars when she spoke or laughed. Young men for miles around had begged for her hand in marriage, but Thi Kinh refused them all, preferring to marry a poor and simple man from her own village.

Thi Kinh worked in the rice fields by day and attended to her household chores at night. It was a hard life, but Thi Kinh didn't mind the endless toil. Because she loved her home and her husband with all her heart she was content.

One afternoon Thi Kinh was sitting outdoors shelling shrimp for the evening meal, while her husband napped in a hammock.

Thi Kinh gazed fondly at her husband. And then she noticed that one of the hairs in his beard was growing in the wrong direction. She went into the hut and got a

sharp knife. Then Thi Kinh tiptoed over to where her husband lay and bent over him, intending to shave off the hair while he slept.

Just then Thi Kinh's husband stirred in his sleep. The knife slipped and scratched his cheek, and he awoke with a start. When he saw Thi Kinh standing over him and holding a knife, he leaped to his feet in alarm.

"You were trying to murder me!" he screamed at the astonished Thi Kinh. "Murderess! Leave my house at once!"

Thi Kinh was so surprised by her husband's angry words that she was unable to speak. But several neighbors heard the commotion and came running to see what was the matter.

24

"Thi Kinh tried to kill me!" her husband told them. "Look at the knife! There's blood on it!"

Shamed by her husband's awful accusation, Thi Kinh bowed her head and began to weep. Her silence and her tears seemed to prove that what her husband was saying was indeed the truth, and Thi Kinh was told to leave the village and never to return.

Homeless and friendless, Thi Kinh trudged through the countryside. She did not know where she ought to go or what she ought to do. When she could walk no longer, she lay down beneath a tree and wept until she fell asleep.

The next day Thi Kinh came upon an old pagoda which had become a monastery. Thi Kinh stood very still and watched the brown-robed monks go about their busi-

25

ness of meditation and prayer. The peace and the beauty of life in the monastery soothed Thi Kinh's aching heart, and she decided to disguise herself as a man and seek refuge within the monastery's walls.

She cut off her long hair, rubbed her smooth face with dirt, and rearranged her clothes. Then she went to the gates of the monastery and begged for admittance. Not realizing that she was a woman, the Superior of the monastery welcomed her and bade her stay as long as she wished.

Life was slow and peaceful within the monastery. As the days passed, Thi Kinh began to forget the trouble and heartbreak that had brought her to the monastery. She kept to herself and never spoke. None of the other monks suspected that she was a woman.

26

Several years later a baby was left upon the steps of
the pagoda. The baby's mother was so poor that she could
no longer afford to care for the child, so she had wrapped
it in a ragged blanket and abandoned it to the charity of
the monks.

When the motherless infant opened its eyes and saw
the cluster of brown-robed monks peering down at it, it
began to cry. Thi Kinh alone understood that the baby

was frightened of the monks and wanted its mother. She knelt and cradled the child in her arms, crooning to it until it stopped crying and nestled against her shoulder.

The other monks stared at her in horror for now they realized that she was a woman.

The Superior of the monastery was very angry at having been tricked by Thi Kinh. He ordered her to take the baby and leave the monastery within the hour. Thi Kinh had no choice but to obey.

Although Thi Kinh was so unhappy that she no longer cared what became of her, she knew that the baby depended upon her for its food and shelter. And she did all that she could. She trudged from village to village, working in the fields, gathering firewood, and sometimes beg-

28

ging from door to door so as to get enough food for the child.

The long weeks of hunger, worry, grief, and wandering took their toll. Thi Kinh's beauty faded. Her lustrous black hair became gray. Her smooth cheeks and forehead were lined. Her once-sparkling eyes grew dull. She was thin and ragged.

29

At last her roaming brought her to the outskirts of the village where she had lived with her husband years ago. She was so changed that no one recognized her as she walked slowly down the street, holding a begging-bowl in one hand and the baby in the other.

A man came forward and dropped several coins into the bowl.

"You remind me of someone I loved," he said sadly, when Thi Kinh thanked him for his generosity. "I give you this in her name."

Thi Kinh stared at him. It was her husband!

"I had a wife named Thi Kinh," he continued. "I drove her away with my false accusations, and I have regretted it ever since. Oh, what I wouldn't give to see her again!"

30

Tears filled Thi Kinh's eyes, and her hands shook so that she could hardly hold the bowl. In a halting voice she told her husband who she was and all that had happened since she'd left the village.

When she had finished, her husband took the begging-bowl from her hands and smashed it to the ground.

"You will never have to beg again," he told her.

For at last Thi Kinh had come home.

Many years later Thi Kinh's story reached the ears of the King. He was so impressed by her courage and her goodness that he bestowed upon her the title of Quan-Am Tong-Tu, which means The Compassionate Protector of Children.

And so she is remembered to this day.

31

THE
GENII
OF THE
HEARTH

Long ago a man named Trong Cao lived with his wife Thi Nhi in a little village that overlooked the great Red River. They were very poor. Every day Trong Cao worked in the rice paddies and Thi Nhi scrubbed and cooked and sewed from dawn to dusk. Yet despite their poverty Trong Cao and Thi Nhi were happy with their life together.

And then one autumn the waters of the Red River rose so high that they overflowed their banks. The entire countryside was flooded with muddy, yellow water. All of the carefully tended crops were ruined. Many huts were washed away. When the waters receded, there was neither work nor food for any man, woman, or child in Trong Cao's village. And so one by one the villagers trudged off to seek their fortunes elsewhere.

Trong Cao and his wife knew that it would be very difficult for them both to find work in the same place. After many tears and promises, they parted. Trong Cao went north. Thi Nhi went south.

Thi Nhi wandered for many weeks. At last she came to the villa of a retired mandarin whose name was Pham Lang. Pham Lang's wife had died, and now he needed someone to keep his house and cook his meals. When he heard that Thi Nhi was looking for work, Pham Lang sought her out and offered her a job in his home. Scarcely able to believe in her good luck, Thi Nhi eagerly accepted the mandarin's generous offer.

Pham Lang was as wise and witty as he was wealthy, and Thi Nhi soon became very fond of him. She had fine

34

clothes to wear and as much to eat as she wanted. But despite her good fortune, Thi Nhi never forgot her beloved Trong Cao.

Whenever a stranger came to the villa, Thi Nhi asked if he had heard any word of a man named Trong Cao. Many beggars passed through the village, but none of them had ever met Thi Nhi's lost husband. She began to despair. And then one day a beggar from the north came to Pham Lang's door to beg for alms.

Thi Nhi filled the beggar's chipped bowl with hot rice. "Have you ever met a man named Trong Cao?" she asked.

To Thi Nhi's surprise the beggar nodded. "Yes," he said. "I remember a man, in a village far to the north. He said that his name was Trong Cao, and he was searching for his wife. But he was very ill, and I believe that he died."

Thi Nhi cried out. She fell upon the floor and beat

35

her fists against the cobblestones until they bled. When Pham Lang found out what had happened, he ordered his other servants to carry Thi Nhi to her room and put her to bed.

For three days and three nights Thi Nhi did not stir. She neither ate nor drank. She lay on her back and stared up at the ceiling. Tears welled constantly in her eyes and streamed down her sunken cheeks.

"My heart is broken," she told Pham Lang. "I do not want to live."

Pham Lang knew that Thi Nhi had loved her husband, and so he was gentle with her. He brought her tempting bits of food and coaxed her to eat.

"I know how you feel," he would console her. "I know how terrible it is to lose a loved one. Didn't I lose my own dear wife just as you've lost your husband?"

Little by little Thi Nhi's heart began to mend. She rose from her bed and tried to go about her duties. Pham Lang saw to it that her tasks were light and that her days were filled with beauty and song. He bade her walk through his gardens. He read poetry to her. He ordered jade bangles for her ears and wrists.

At last Thi Nhi was able to forget her bitter sorrow. But there were always moments when she would stop whatever it was that she was doing and stare up at the sky, remembering Trong Cao and the happiness they had known together.

Pham Lang had always admired Thi Nhi, and Thi Nhi had grown very fond of Pham Lang during the years that she had spent in his household. She was not surprised, then, when the retired mandarin asked her if she would be his wife. Although she knew that a part of her soul would always belong to Trong Cao, Thi Nhi agreed to marry Pham Lang.

Their marriage was a happy one. Pham Lang spared no cost or effort in his attempt to make his new bride's life happy, and Thi Nhi was proud to be the wife of so rich and respected a man as Pham Lang.

One afternoon Pham Lang went off to hunt in the forest. Thi Nhi stayed home alone. The day grew gray, and Thi Nhi gazed idly out the window at the clouds that scudded across the darkening sky. For the first time in many months, her thoughts dwelt upon her lost Trong Cao. Sudden tears brimmed in her eyes.

There was a rap at the door. Blinking back her tears, Thi Nhi hurried to see who was there.

"Alms," said the beggar who knelt before her in the yard. "Please, have you a bit of rice that you can spare?"

The beggar's voice sent a chill down Thi Nhi's spine. Suddenly she could hardly breathe. She peered closely at the ragged beggar and realized that it was none other than Trong Cao, her long-lost husband!

Husband and wife stood there and stared at each other. They were hardly able to believe their eyes, for each had long since given the other up for dead.

Shaking so that she could scarcely walk, Thi Nhi led Trong Cao into the warm kitchen. She cleared a place for him at the table. After she'd given him a heaping bowl of meat and rice, she brewed a pot of strong tea for him to drink. When Trong Cao had finished eating, Thi Nhi fetched some of Pham Lang's clothes for him.

Trong Cao told Thi Nhi of all that had befallen him. He had not been fortunate. Blizzards had swept the northern villages, and he had become so seriously ill that all had given him up for dead. Although he'd recovered from his sickness, it had left him so thin and so weak that he could not work and so he had been forced to beg for his living.

Fresh tears ran down Thi Nhi's face as she listened to her husband's tale. Still weeping she told Trong Cao that she had found work here in Pham Lang's villa and that she had finally married Pham Lang because a beggar from the north had told her that Trong Cao was dead.

There was the sound of footfalls in the yard. Pham Lang was returning. Fear clutched at Thi Nhi's heart. Pham Lang was a good man, but he had a quick temper.

40

What would he do if he walked into his kitchen and found his wife with another man?

"Quickly!" she told Trong Cao. "Go out through the back door and hide in that stack of straw by the barn. I'll give Pham Lang his dinner and see to it that he's in a good mood, and then we'll talk everything over and see what's to be done!"

Husband and wife embraced. Then Trong Cao ran outdoors and crept under the stack of straw.

Pham Lang came into the kitchen and hugged his wife.

"Your dinner is ready," said Thi Nhi. "Will you have it now?"

"In a minute," said Pham Lang. "I want to prepare those ashes so that they'll be ready to spread on the fields tomorrow morning. I'll be right back."

Thi Nhi was so dazed by Trong Cao's miraculous return that she scarcely heard Pham Lang's words.

Pham Lang went out into the backyard. He lit a taper and set fire to the stack of straw so that its ashes would be ready for the fields in the morning. A strong wind fanned the flames, and the whole stack of straw was ablaze by the time Thi Nhi realized what was happening.

"Trong Cao!" screamed Thi Nhi, running out of the house. "Oh, my beloved! Wait for me!"

And she leaped into the flames.

Only then did Pham Lang understand what had happened.

"Thi Nhi," he cried. "Wait! I will save you! I will save both of you!"

And he too plunged into the fire.

When the spirits of Trong Cao, Thi Nhi, and Pham Lang stood together before the Jade Emperor and told him their sad history, he was so moved that he wept.

"Such true love deserves a reward," said the Jade Emperor. "All of Vietnam shall remember you and honor you. Pham Lang, I appoint you Genie of the Kitchen. Trong Cao, you shall be Genie of the Earth. And Thi Nhi, you shall be the Genie in charge of recording the births and marriages of each family."

And to this very day the spirits of the three Genii of the Hearth live snugly upon the hearth of every home in Vietnam.

43

THE
JEWELED
SLIPPER

Ong Ba had two daughters. Their names were Cam and Tam.

Cam was sweet, slight, and merry as a hearth-cricket, and her disposition was as lovely as her face. Her bright black eyes sparkled when she spoke or laughed, and even her nose had a happy tilt to it.

Tam might have been a pretty girl had she tried to smile now and then, but she never did. She was short and fat and homely, and she envied her beautiful younger sister with all her heart.

One day Ong Ba decided that he fancied a platter of fried fish for supper. He bade Cam and Tam run and find their buckets and fishing nets.

"I will give a beautiful jade necklace to whoever catches more fish," promised Ong Ba.

The two sisters hurried to the village pond and cast their nets. Although Cam caught more fish, Tam was determined to have the jade necklace for herself.

"Look!" exclaimed Tam, pointing toward the far side of the pond. "Look at that beautiful white lotus-flower! You've already got so many fish, Cam, why don't you wade across and pick it so we can take it home to our father."

Cam immediately laid down her fishing net and waded across the pond to pick the lotus-flower. But when she returned, her bucket was empty and Tam was gone. Realizing that her sister had tricked her, Cam began to weep.

Suddenly a genie appeared at her side. "Soon you'll live in a golden palace and be married to a prince," the

genie told Cam. "Stop crying now, and listen to what I say. There's a little blue fish in your bucket. Take him home with you, and take good care of him. And you will see what you see."

So saying, the genie disappeared.

To Cam's astonishment, there *was* a tiny blue fish swimming at the bottom of her bucket. Cam took the fish home and put him in a glass bowl. Ong Ba had already given the jade necklace to Tam, but Cam was so happy with her little blue fish that she didn't complain about her sister's dishonesty.

Even though she'd managed to get the jade necklace for herself, Tam wasn't happy. Cam was still much more beautiful than she was, and now Cam had a little blue fish to play with. Tam waited until Cam went out to

47

gather wood, and then she killed the little blue fish and buried its bones beneath a big areca tree.

When Cam came home and saw that her little blue fish was gone, she was so unhappy that she went to bed without supper and cried herself to sleep.

At the hour before dawn, a strange rooster crowed beneath Cam's window.

> Cock-a-doodle-doo
> A fish that was blue
> Give me some grain
> And I'll show him to you.

Cam hurried to give the rooster a handful of grain. After he'd gobbled up all the grain, the rooster led Cam to the areca tree and told her to dig a hole. When Cam

48

found the bones of her little blue fish, she sank to her knees and wept with despair.

"Crying again?" asked the genie, who had appeared in the areca tree. "Wipe your face and pay attention to what I say. Bury the bones of your little blue fish beneath your bed. Wait a hundred days, and then dig them up, and remember that soon you'll live in a golden palace and be married to a prince."

And the genie disappeared.

Cam did as the genie had told her to do. She wrapped the bones in a bit of silk and buried them under her bed. A hundred days passed. But when Cam tried to dig up the bones, she found that they had vanished and in their place was a pair of lovely jeweled slippers.

49

Cam had never seen such slippers! They were decorated with rows of emeralds, jade, rubies, and diamonds. They were stitched round with golden thread and laced with beaten silver. They were so beautiful that Cam no longer wept for her little blue fish.

All the other girls in the village begged to try on the jeweled slippers, but the slippers fit no one but Cam. Even Tam was unable to wear them.

Cam was delighted with her jeweled slippers, and she wore them every day. But one morning while she was working in Ong Ba's rice paddies, a black crow snatched up one of her slippers in his beak and flew away with it.

It wasn't long before the crow grew tired of carrying the slipper and dropped it. And it so happened that Cam's jeweled slipper landed right in the middle of the King's royal gardens!

50

The next morning the King's son discovered the little slipper. He didn't know how it had come to be in his father's gardens, but he was certain that the girl who wore such an exquisite slipper must be the loveliest girl in the kingdom.

"I will find her and marry her," said the King's son.

Messengers were dispatched to all parts of the country to announce that the King's son wished to marry the girl whose foot fit the beautiful jeweled slipper that he had found in his father's garden. Many girls came to the palace, but the little slipper fit none of them. The Prince began to despair.

At last Cam came forward. As soon as she slid her foot into the jeweled slipper, the Prince announced that he had found his bride.

When Tam heard of her sister's good fortune, she was furious. The very idea of Cam marrying a prince and

51

living in a golden palace was enough to make the envious Tam weep with rage.

"Marry the Prince, will she?" muttered Tam. "Not if *I* can stop her!"

The day before the wedding was to take place, Tam approached her sister.

"I saw some beautiful flowers growing in the forest," said Tam. "They'd be perfect for your bridal garland, sister. Shall I go with you and show you where to find them?"

The unsuspecting Cam agreed, and the sisters set off together. Soon they were deep in the forest. Suddenly Tam turned and struck Cam on the head with a stout stick. Cam fell to the ground, and Tam ran away.

52

Cam lay in the forest all night long. At dawn an old woman found her. The old woman carried Cam to her hut and nursed her until she was well again.

Although Cam soon recovered from the cruel blow she had received from her sister, she could not remember who she was or what had happened to her. She remained with the old woman for many months.

The Prince had never stopped searching for his lost bride. Even though the King urged him to forget about Cam and to choose another for his wife, the Prince remained faithful. He would have the girl whose foot had fit the jeweled slipper and no one else.

One day the Prince was hunting in the forest. He was thirsty, and he stopped at the old woman's door to ask if he might have a cup of tea. The old woman told him to sit down, and then Cam brought in the tea and set it before him.

"My beloved bride!" cried the Prince. "I've found you at last! But what are you doing here? Why did you run away?"

Cam stared at him. She was too astonished to say a word.

Seeing her look of confusion, the Prince reached into his tunic and pulled out the little jeweled slipper. When she saw the slipper, Cam's memory came flooding back and she remembered who she was and all that had happened to her.

The Prince rewarded the old woman handsomely.

54

Then he set Cam upon his horse and carried her back to the palace. The next day they were married.

Now that Cam was a princess, Tam hoped for special favors.

"Dearest sister," said Tam. "You are married, but I am not. Please, tell me your secret. How is it that your skin is always so smooth and soft?"

But Cam was no longer deceived by Tam's false flattery. "I always bathe in boiling water," Cam told Tam. "It does wonders for your skin, you know."

Hurrying to the kitchen, Tam leaped head first into a vat of boiling water, and that was the last anyone ever saw of her.

But Cam and her prince lived happily ever after in the golden palace just as the genie had promised.

THE
MAGIC
CRYSTAL

Mi Nuong was the daughter of a very wealthy mandarin. She lived in a magnificent palace that overlooked a river and was surrounded by lovely gardens filled with blooming flowers and shaded by gentle willow trees.

Mi Nuong was as beautiful as her surroundings. She was a slender, graceful girl, and she loved to dance and sing in her father's gardens. Her long black eyelashes fluttered prettily when she spoke, and her smiling mouth was like a small and perfect lotus-flower.

Mi Nuong's appearance gave happiness to all who beheld her. Even the elements paid loving homage to her. The sun shone with a special brightness when Mi Nuong came to her window. The willows in the garden bent their branches to her dancing, and the wild birds sang as sweetly as they could when they glimpsed Mi Nuong's face.

On the day after her sixteenth birthday, Mi Nuong heard a wonderful voice. Beyond the walls of her father's palace, a mysterious stranger was rowing his little sampan along the river. Mi Nuong could not see his face, for he was too far away. Nonetheless the river breeze carried the stranger's voice to Mi Nuong's window, and she realized that the stranger was singing the most beautiful song she had ever heard.

Mi Nuong leaned far out of her window so that she would not miss a single note. The song made her think of moonlight in a faraway land; it rippled with the joy of a thousand mountain streams; it whispered of the morning mists upon the sea. It was a song that celebrated the beauty of the seasons, the sweetness of the woods-flowers, the breathless glory of the sun and moon and

58

stars. It was a song of praise and thanks and love, and tears of wonder filled Mi Nuong's eyes as she listened.

The stranger's little sampan drifted slowly down the river, and his voice faded away. At last he was no more than a speck in the distance, and Mi Nuong could no longer hear him. She sighed and moved slowly away from the window.

Mi Nuong did not sleep that night. The words of the stranger's song rang in her ears, and she gave herself up to imagining what sort of man the stranger might be.

He is tall and handsome, thought Mi Nuong. He is strong and noble and true, and he will carry me away to a golden palace and make me his bride!

Mi Nuong could hardly wait for morning. As soon

as the first ray of sunshine lightened the sky, she posted herself by her window to wait for the mysterious stranger.

But he did not return.

Day after day Mi Nuong sat at her window. She no longer cared for her beautiful books, her silken gowns, her jewels, or her other amusements. Her handmaidens tried to distract her, but it was no use. Mi Nuong lingered at her window and gazed out over the treetops at the river, waiting for the stranger who never came again.

Mi Nuong became more unhappy with every day that passed. She could think of nothing but the mysterious stranger and his song, and she yearned to meet him face to face. She dreamed of being his bride, for although she had never seen him save from her window, Mi Nuong was hopelessly in love with him.

60

The weeks passed. Mi Nuong despaired. She grew thin and pale, for she never ventured out of her room. Her eyes lost their brightness. Her gleaming hair became limp and dull. Mi Nuong could neither eat nor sleep, and at last she grew dangerously ill.

The Mandarin summoned the finest doctors, but none of them could tell the Mandarin what was wrong with Mi Nuong. Meanwhile, Mi Nuong became weaker and weaker, and her wide eyes became sadder and sadder in her pale face.

Mi Nuong's father was frantic with worry. He feared that his daughter would die. At last he summoned all of Mi Nuong's handmaidens before him and asked if any one of them knew what was wrong with Mi Nuong.

The youngest of the handmaidens stepped timidly forward and knelt before the Mandarin.

61

"Please," said the little handmaiden. "On the day after Mi Nuong's sixteenth birthday, a mysterious stranger in a sampan came rowing by. He was singing, and never before have I heard so lovely a song!" The little handmaiden's eyes lit up at the memory of it.

"Mi Nuong was quite enchanted," continued the little handmaiden. "She lingered at her window long after the stranger had sailed away, and she has waited for him ever since. But he has never come back, and so Mi Nuong grieves for him."

The Mandarin was amazed. "Can it be merely a fisherman's song that has made my daughter so ill?" he asked.

"It is possible," said the doctors.

"And can it be that my daughter is love-sick?" questioned the Mandarin.

62

"It is possible," repeated the doctors.

"Fetch this fisherman who sings so wonderfully!" the Mandarin commanded his servants. "Bring him to the palace. If Mi Nuong wants him, she shall have him!"

The Mandarin's servants made inquiries throughout the town. They were directed to the little hut of a poor fisherman named Trong Chi. When the Mandarin's servants explained their errand, Trong Chi gladly accompanied them to the palace. He was but a poor man, and he was greatly honored by the Mandarin's summons.

Trong Chi gaped with amazement and awe as he was led through the gates and into the Mandarin's palace. He passed through hall after hall of gold and jade and silver, and his mouth dropped a little farther open with each new treasure that he beheld. He was a simple, plain man, and he had never dreamed that such riches could exist under a single roof.

At last Trong Chi was brought into the bedroom where Mi Nuong lay propped among the pillows. At the sight of Mi Nuong's grace and delicate features, Trong Chi fell to his knees and vowed that he would love this beautiful maiden for the rest of his life. Trong Chi's heart filled with love for the Mandarin's daughter, and his heart was so full of love and hope and joy that he could not utter a single word.

Mi Nuong raised herself on one elbow so that she might see the mysterious stranger of whom she'd dreamed for so many weeks. But instead of the tall and handsome prince that she'd imagined, she beheld only a lowly fisherman with bare feet and ragged clothes.

Is this the man I've shed so many tears for? Mi Nuong asked herself. And she laughed out loud of the very thought of being in love with such a sorry-looking man.

In that moment Mi Nuong's lovesickness was cured.
Sadly Trong Chi made his way back to his hut by
the edge of the river. Mi Nuong had rejected him, but
his love for her remained. He knew that no matter how
long he lived, he would never forget the Mandarin's
lovely daughter.

Tears streamed down his poor, thin cheeks. His
heart ached with love for the beautiful Mi Nuong, but
she was the daughter of a wealthy mandarin and he was
only a poor fisherman. What right had he to be in love
with her?

Trong Chi knew that he would probably never see
Mi Nuong again. His sorrow was too much for him to

bear. He lay down upon his cot, turned his face to the wall, and then his heart broke in half and he died.

When Trong Chi's fellow fishermen came to look for him the next day, they found only a crystal. Trong Chi had vanished.

One of the fishermen took the crystal home with him and carved it into a lovely little teacup.

Back at the palace Mi Nuong had begun to regret her laughter of the day before. She was a good and generous girl, and she wished that she had behaved more kindly to poor Trong Chi. But Trong Chi had vanished, and there was nothing to be done.

The weeks came and went, and at last it was time for the Mandarin's annual festival. On this day the gates

of the palace were thrown open to all the peasants of the town. There was food and drink for everyone, and many of the peasants presented gifts to the Mandarin and his family.

One of the gifts was the exquisite teacup that Trong Chi's friend had carved from the crystal he'd found in Trong Chi's hut.

Mi Nuong was entranced with the little teacup. She turned it over and over in her hands and then announced that she would keep it forever.

That night the teacup was filled with fragrant tea. But as soon as Mi Nuong raised the cup to her lips, something quite extraordinary happened. Trong Chi's face appeared in the bottom of the cup!

68

Mi Nuong gazed at the magic image in astonishment. She remembered how sweetly Trong Chi had sung and how filled with devotion his eyes had been on that day when she'd laughed at him. She realized that Trong Chi was dead but that his spirit loved her still and so was not able to rest.

At this thought a tear of remorse rolled down Mi Nuong's soft cheek and fell into the teacup. And at that very instant the teacup vanished.

Trong Chi's love for Mi Nuong had been so great and so pure that a single tear from Mi Nuong's lovely eyes had been able to set his restless spirit at peace. The debt of love had been paid, and the magic crystal had disappeared forever.

THE
SHADOW
ON THE
WALL

Me Ne's husband was a soldier. When his battalion was sent away to the northern frontier, Me Ne stayed behind. She kept the house, tilled the rice paddies, took care of her baby son, and longed for the day when her husband would return to her.

Despite the tasks that filled her days, Me Ne missed her husband very much. At night when her work was done and the child lay sleeping in his cradle, Me Ne stood quietly at the window and looked out through the darkness toward the northern frontier. Her eyes swam with tears, and her lips moved in a fervent prayer for her husband's safe return.

The long summer months passed, and then it was autumn. Me Ne heard nothing of her husband, and she did not know if he was alive or dead. Winter came, bringing gray skies and cold winds that swept down from the mountains and swirled across the icy fields.

One dark night a particularly terrible storm moved across the land. The wind whistled and moaned around the corners of Me Ne's little hut, and the rain pounded upon the thatched roof. The child was sleeping, and Me Ne sat sewing by the light of a single candle. Suddenly a gust of wind extinguished the candle and at that very instant a loud clap of thunder echoed and re-echoed through the blackness.

The little boy awoke and screamed with terror.

Me Ne plucked the frightened child from his cradle and held him close to her while she relighted the candle. Although the child was somewhat comforted by the familiar flicker of candlelight, he was still very frightened,

and he clung to his mother with all of his might.

"Hush," said Me Ne gently. She pointed to her shadow on the far wall. "Look," she told the child. "There's your daddy. Don't be afraid. Daddy is here, and he will take care of you."

The little boy looked at the shadow and stopped crying. In a few minutes he was asleep.

But the next evening he refused to go to sleep until he had seen his daddy. Me Ne was surprised and delighted. She positioned herself in such a way that her shadow was again cast onto the wall, and her little boy smiled and waved good night to his daddy.

Every night thereafter Me Ne and her little son went through the ceremony of saying good night to Daddy. Me Ne even taught the little boy to clasp his

73

hands and bow to the shadow as he bade it good night.

At last the winter months were over. In April Me Ne's husband returned from the northern frontier.

Me Ne was so overcome with joy at seeing her husband again that she was hardly able to speak. She stood and stared at him for long minutes at a time, and her hands and knees trembled whenever he came near her.

Me Ne's husband was a simple man, and he thought that Me Ne's behavior was a bit strange. He did not understand how very much she loved him and how moved she was at his safe return.

"But aren't we going to have dinner?" he asked at last.

Me Ne bowed and put on her coat and hurried off to the market to buy fresh meat and vegetables for her husband's homecoming feast.

While Me Ne was gone, her husband devoted himself to making friends with the little son whom he had not seen in so many months. But when he told the child who he was, the little boy shook his head and refused to believe it.

"You're not my daddy," said the little boy. "My daddy comes here every night before I go to bed, and I always say good night to him."

Me Ne's husband was shocked and hurt.

This child is too young to have learned how to lie, he thought bitterly. My wife has been deceiving me! There can be no other answer.

When Me Ne returned from the market, she found that her husband was a changed man. He sat in the corner and stared at the fire and would not speak to her. He refused to drink the tea she brewed for him, and he

turned his face away from the festive supper that Me Ne prepared.

Poor Me Ne was at her wits' end. "Won't you tell me what is wrong?" she pleaded.

But her husband turned his face to the wall and would not say a word.

Me Ne burst into tears and ran from the house.

Me Ne's husband did not know what to make of Me Ne's outburst. He began to wonder if he had not somehow been mistaken about his wife's loyalty. He decided that he would question her as soon as she returned, and settle the matter one way or the other.

Several hours passed. But Me Ne did not return.

It had become dark. Me Ne's husband prepared the child for bed and lit the candle.

"There's my daddy!" cried the little boy. He clasped his little hands and bowed to the husband's shadow on the wall. "Good night, Daddy," said the child. And he bowed once more to the shadow on the wall.

Now Me Ne's husband understood everything. He was terribly ashamed of himself.

"I have been jealous of a shadow," he groaned.

In the meantime Me Ne had come back. Watching through the window, she'd seen everything. But she was a good Vietnamese wife, and she loved her husband with all her heart. She knew that it would not be wise to shame him by making it seem that he had behaved foolishly. At the same time she wanted him to know that things were all right between them. She walked slowly into the hut.

"Will you have your dinner now?" she asked her husband softly.

And as easily as that, she forgave him for being jealous of a mere shadow on the wall.

77

THE DESTINY OF PRINCESS TIEN DUNG

King Hung Vuong had but a single daughter, a graceful girl whose name was Tien Dung. This Princess was both beautiful and accomplished, and as she grew to womanhood she was courted by every young prince and king and mandarin for miles around. Dozens of wealthy suitors traveled to King Vuong's palace each month to plead for Tien Dung's hand in marriage, but the beautiful Princess refused them all.

"It is not time for me to marry," she told her father. "Let me enjoy my girlhood for just a few more years. I feel that my destiny will be a special one. When the time is right, destiny will provide me with a husband."

The King was so fond of his only daughter that he allowed her to have her own way. All of the hopeful suitors were turned away. Princess Tien Dung filled her

days with long walks, sumptuous picnics and pleasant excursions through the lovely hills and valleys of her father's vast kingdom.

One warm summer's day Princess Tien Dung decided that she would like to visit the ancient pagoda that stood just south of the village of Chu-Xa. Accordingly the Princess and her ladies clambered onto the royal barges and set sail down the river to Chu-Xa. The trip was a long one, and it was late afternoon when they arrived at their destination.

It was as magnificent a spot as Tien Dung could have wished. The white beach sloped gently away from the river, and the leaves of the green palm and bamboo fanned breezes into the sunshine. Princess Tien Dung sighed with delight and ordered her servants to unload the baskets of food.

The late afternoon sun was especially warm, and it

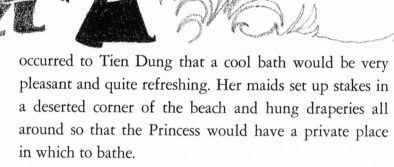

occurred to Tien Dung that a cool bath would be very pleasant and quite refreshing. Her maids set up stakes in a deserted corner of the beach and hung draperies all around so that the Princess would have a private place in which to bathe.

When everything was ready, Princess Tien Dung slipped behind the curtains, took off her clothes, and prepared to wade into the cool, clear water.

And then she stopped and stared, scarcely able to believe her eyes. At the very edge of the water, in a deep hollow that had not been visible before, lay a young man . . . and he was completely naked! The astonished princess blushed and blushed until it seemed that her face had caught fire. She did not know whether she ought to run away or close her eyes or scream for her ladies-in-waiting. But the first thing she did was to snatch up a chemise and wrap it about herself.

81

Embarrassed at being discovered, the young man hastened to explain.

"My name is Chu Dong Tu," he told her. "My mother died when I was small, and I lived with my father in a tiny hut on the bank of this river. We were very poor, but we got along until one day our little hut burned to the ground and left us with nothing but a single pair of trousers between us.

"We took turns wearing the trousers, but then my father became very ill. He knew that he was dying, and with his last breath he told me to bury him naked and to keep the trousers for myself. But I could not bring myself to do such a dishonorable thing, and so you see me as I am, with not even a loincloth to my name."

Princess Tien Dung wept to think of such poverty. "But how do you manage to live?" she asked him.

82

"I fish at night when it is so dark that nobody can see me. In the morning I wade out into the river so that the water rises above my waist, and I sell my catch of fish to the travelers whose boats pass here.

"When I saw your royal barges decked with flowers and banners, I hid myself as well as I could in this hollow. But now you have found me."

Tien Dung gazed thoughtfully at the young man who now stood before her. Chu Dong Tu was handsome and well-built and much more interesting than the princes and kings and mandarins with whom Tien Dung had always been acquainted. She decided that this peculiar encounter could only be an act of fate, and that she was destined to be the wife of Chu Dong Tu.

"We will be married," Tien Dung told the astounded young peasant.

Tien Dung called to her servants and told them to bring some trousers and a vest for Chu Dong Tu. She then led Chu Dong Tu to the royal barge and bade him eat and drink. There was a great feast, and the wedding of Princess Tien Dung to the peasant Chu Dong Tu took place that very same night.

When King Hung Vuong was informed of his daughter's marriage, he flew into a terrible rage. How dare the headstrong Tien Dung marry without his royal permission? And how dare she marry a penniless peasant? The King was so angry that he banished both his daughter and her lowborn husband forever.

The shocking news spread rapidly through the kingdom. Tien Dung and her husband were outcasts. They trudged from village to village, but no one dared to offer so much as a bowl of rice to the unfortunate pair.

Chu Dong Tu was frightened and discouraged, but Tien Dung trusted in her special destiny and refused to despair.

After three days of wandering, Tien Dung and Chu Dong Tu came upon a crumbling pagoda standing all by itself in the midst of a forest. The pagoda was inhabited by an old hermit who had never heard of King Hung Vuong or of his daughter. The hermit welcomed the weary pair and told them that they might stay with him for as long as they wished.

Tien Dung and Chu Dong Tu spent several pleasant weeks with the old hermit. Upon their departure the hermit insisted upon giving each of them a gift. Chu Dong Tu received a bamboo walking stick, and there was a conical-shaped hat made of woven palm leaves for Tien Dung.

After a long day of walking, Tien Dung and Chu Dong Tu found themselves in a bare and barren country that was strange to them. Fortunately the sky was clear and they were able to make their bed upon the open ground. Chu Dong Tu drove the bamboo walking stick into the ground, and Tien Dung hung her conical-shaped hat upon it for safekeeping. Then they both lay down to sleep.

When they awoke the next morning, they discovered that the bamboo walking stick and the hat made of woven palm leaves had been miraculously transformed into a marvelous walled citadel. Chu Dong Tu was speechless with amazement, but Tien Dung merely smiled. "I always knew that my destiny would be a special one," she said.

86

There was a fabulous palace within the citadel. Its walls were solid gold, its lofty ceilings were fifty feet high and made of beaten silver, and its floors were composed of diamonds and rubies set in fantastic geometric patterns and bordered with strips of the rarest jade. The palace was staffed by hundreds of admiring and obedient servants who brought Tien Dung and Chu Dong Tu fine new clothes, platter upon platter of every food and sweetmeat imaginable, and treasure chests filled to the brim with gold coins and delicate ivory carvings.

People came from all over the kingdom to marvel at this remarkable citadel and at the incredible palace of riches that stood within its walls.

But when King Hung Vuong heard about the citadel, he was angrier than ever. How dare his disobedient daugh-

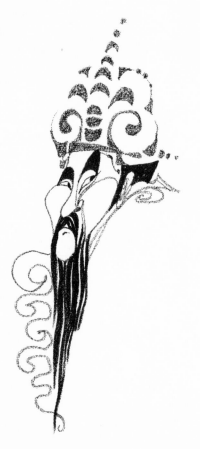

ter and her peasant husband set up a walled citadel in the middle of his kingdom!

"This is treason!" bellowed the King.

He called his generals and prepared to send his entire army against Tien Dung and Chu Dong Tu.

Chu Dong Tu wanted to fight the King. But Tien Dung refused.

"I did not build this citadel," she told Chu Dong Tu. "And neither did you. Heaven built these walls, and if Heaven wants them to be defended, Heaven will defend them. As for me, I will not defy my father. Our destiny is a special one, and we must trust Heaven."

That evening the King's army arrived at the citadel. It was too dark to attack, so the soldiers pitched their camp upon the slopes of a nearby hill to wait for sunrise.

88

Tien Dung did not fear her father's army. "Let us enjoy ourselves while we can," she said with a laugh.

And so there was feasting and dancing and music and revelry within the citadel, and the merrymaking went on until midnight.

At the stroke of twelve a mysterious whirlwind swirled up out of nowhere and enveloped the citadel and all within its walls in clouds of glowing dust. In less than a moment the entire citadel was blown up to Heaven to remain forever in the immortal court of the Jade Emperor.

All that was left of the wondrous walled citadel was a large blue lake. And to this day Vietnamese girls wander along the shores of the lake and think about the Princess Tien Dung and her special destiny in the court of the Jade Emperor.

THE
SILVER
RIVER

Chuc Nu was the youngest and the prettiest of the Jade Emperor's daughters. Although many of her sisters were married, Chuc Nu remained a maiden. She was a nimble-fingered, intelligent girl, and the Jade Emperor set her to weaving new clothes for his subjects. Chuc Nu's loom stood so close to the Silver River that the sounds of her shuttle mingled with the sounds of the Silver River's waves to make a gentle, soothing music. Day after day Chuc Nu wove and sang beside the lovely Silver River. She loved her work and was quite contented.

The Silver River flows through the center of the Jade Emperor's celestial kingdom. It is very wide. Those who live on the Earth know it as a vast band of stars called the Milky Way. But in the Jade Emperor's kingdom, it is called the Silver River.

91

One day a young shepherd came to the edge of the river to water his flock. When he saw Chuc Nu sitting at her loom, he bowed and introduced himself as Nguu Lang, the imperial shepherd. They met every day thereafter. Nguu Lang was fascinated by the lovely little maiden who sang so joyously and worked so diligently at her loom, and Chuc Nu thought that the youthful shepherd was the strongest and kindest man in her father's kingdom.

It was not long before the two young people realized that they were in love. They immediately sought out the Jade Emperor and asked for permission to marry.

"Love is not everything," the Jade Emperor told them. "Both of you have very important tasks to perform in my kingdom."

Chuc Nu and Nguu Lang hung their heads.

"Very well," said the Jade Emperor. "If you give me your word that your loom and your flocks will not be neglected, I will allow you to wed."

Chuc Nu and Nguu Lang hastened to assure the Jade Emperor that they would continue to work at their tasks, and Chuc Nu became Nguu Lang's wife in a lovely ceremony attended by all the lords and ladies of the Jade Emperor's celestial court.

Now that they were man and wife, the happiness of Chuc Nu and Nguu Lang was so great that it bewitched them. Chuc Nu forgot all about her loom, and Nguu Lang let his sheep stray. They had eyes only for each other, and they were so much in love that they were aware of nothing outside themselves.

It was not long before Chuc Nu's loom was covered with dust and cobwebs. The Jade Emperor's subjects had to make do with their old clothes, and the imperial sheep ran wild and ate all the flowers in the imperial gardens.

Angrily the Jade Emperor warned Chuc Nu and Nguu Lang to mend their ways. The two young people were contrite and apologetic, but no sooner had they left the Jade Emperor's presence than they forgot every word that he'd said to them. Chuc Nu's loom continued to stand idle, and Nguu Lang's sheep continued to wander where they pleased.

At last the Jade Emperor lost his temper. He ordered Chuc Nu to return to her loom, and he sent Nguu Lang to herd sheep on the far side of the Silver River.

It seemed that Chuc Nu and Nguu Lang would be separated forever.

94

However Chuc Nu wept so bitterly at the loss of her beloved Nguu Lang that the Jade Emperor relented, and now husband and wife are allowed to meet for one week each year, during the month of Ngau.

At this time of year all the crows seem to vanish from the Vietnamese countryside. It is said that they have all flown away to the Jade Emperor's celestial kingdom, so that they may join their wings together and form a bridge across the Silver River for Chuc Nu and Nguu Lang.

ABOUT THE AUTHOR

Gail B. Graham has worked as a free-lance writer and reporter. Her travels range from the Virgin Islands and pre-Castro Cuba to Hong Kong and Japan. She has also spent two six-week periods in Vietnam; one in 1966 and one in 1967 when she was captured by the Viet Cong. An article she wrote while there was read into the *Congressional Record.* It was also during these visits that she spent hours in Saigon libraries and bookstalls researching Vietnamese fairy tales and folklore. The stories chosen for this collection are her favorites.

Mrs. Graham, who now lives in California with her husband and two children, is the author of THE LITTLE BROWN GAZELLE, written under the name Gail Barclay.

ABOUT THE ARTIST

Brigitte Bryan was born in Germany in 1938. She studied art in Wiesbaden and Munich and has worked all over Europe at various jobs in free-lance design and magazine illustration. Since her arrival in the United States in 1966, she has devoted most of her time to illustrating children's books. Among those she has done are THE FOX THAT WANTED NINE GOLDEN TALES and THE KERIS EMERALD.